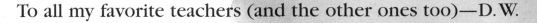

To all my favorite teachers (and the other ones too)—D. W.

To teachers everywhere who can do anything and everything
and to one special teacher at Grant Elementary—D. C.

ISBN 0-439-52809-7

Text copyright © 2002 by Douglas Wood.
Illustrations copyright © 2002 by Doug Cushman. All rights reserved.
Published by Scholastic Inc., 557 Broadway, New York, NY 10012,
by arrangement with Simon & Schuster Books for Young Readers,
Simon & Schuster Children's Publishing Division. SCHOLASTIC
and associated logos are trademarks and/or registered trademarks of Scholastic Inc.

12 11 10 9 8 7 6 5 4 3 2 1   3 4 5 6 7 8/0

Printed in the U.S.A.   08

First Scholastic printing, September 2003

Book design by Greg Stadnyk

The text of this book is set in Garamond.

What Teachers Can't Do

by **Douglas Wood**

pictures by **Doug Cushman**

SCHOLASTIC INC.

New York Toronto London Auckland Sydney
Mexico City New Delhi Hong Kong Buenos Aires

There are lots of things that regular people can do, but teachers can't.

Teachers can't ride skateboards or scooters to school.

They can never be tardy.

Teachers can't buy their own apples.

And they can't teach their best without flowers on their desk.

Teachers can spell "Mississippi" and "encyclopedia."

But they can't spell "CAT."

They can never quite remember what 2 + 2 is, either.

Teachers can't write on the chalkboard without squeaking.

They can't sit in the little chairs, even for story time.

And they can't use the hall pass to go to the bathroom.

Teachers can't cut to the front of the line.

Well . . . okay.

But they aren't allowed to trade desserts.

Teachers *may not* finger paint in their good clothes!

And they can't see out of the backs of their heads. Do you think?

Teachers can't go down the tube slide at recess. . . .

They can twirl but they can't jump.

Teachers can't cry if they skin *their* knees. Can they?

Sometimes teachers forget . . . no snoring during quiet time.

Teachers can't feed the salamander
or guinea pigs by themselves.

And sometimes they need help finding them!

Teachers can never run out of smiles.
Or smiley faces.

Teachers can't wait to come back to school tomorrow.

But first they really need some help cleaning the blackboard.

And the erasers!

No one knows why there are so many things teachers can't do. Maybe because they're so busy doing the thing they do best of all.

Teaching you.